Ruby Leigh

Adventure Series

*Five books on the Adventures of
Ruby Leigh*

by
Grandad
Craig Hookway

Ruby Leigh Adventure Series

Ruby Leigh and Lola go to Villa Park

by Grandad Craig Hookway

Ruby and Lola were bored on a nice sunny morning.

Ruby said "I know, let's go to Villa Park, Grandad is always going on about it." They looked up the time when kick off was, it was 3 o'clock and they were playing Manchester Utd. Ruby put on her Villa kit which

Lola said "Can you stroke me with your magic hands." Ruby said "OK" and sure enough Lola soon got better.

The game started and after only 5 minutes, Villa were losing from somebody called David Beckham from a Free Kick. Villa levelled the score just before half-time by someone called John Mc'Ginn, who seemed to be everywhere on the pitch. The crowd went barmy. Lola was still unsure staying under

Ruby's cardigan, with Ruby jumping up and down with the fans, with Lola clinging on to her

The first half finished, so they went to get some refreshments. Ruby had a chocolate bar and coke, Lola had milk. When they got back to their seat the first half entertainment started. They rolled out a plastic sheet shaped like a football with prizes on it.

The idea is to kick a football onto the sheet and win a prize.

To their amazement Ruby's name was called out. Lola said "Come on let's get Grandad a prize."

When it was Ruby's turn she ran up and gave it the biggest kick she could with her left foot. The ball was going towards the sheet and the crowd started to go Orrrrrrrrrrrrrr Yeh. The ball had landed on a prize. Lola and Ruby looked at

each other and they   just ran to
see what

they had won. (Ruby
thought it may be a
Dress). It was a complete new
Villa Kit. They gave Ruby a
voucher for the Club Shop.
They went back to their seats to a
round of applause feeling
happy and proud of themselves.
The game restarted and United
were awarded a controversial
Penalty! Ruby didn't know
much about football, but that was
clearly a Dive! Lola was now
sitting on Ruby's lap

enjoying herself. She had been singing with the crowd, well some of the words

anyway, and clapping her paws until this happened. That man Beckham went to take the penalty. He drove it towards the corner of the net but within a split second Lola jumped out of Ruby's lap to stop the ball going into the net whereby the Villa Goalkeeper, Tom Heaton could just pick it up. Heaton winked and said "Thank you"

One of the fans saw
Lola's name on her
collar. The crowd
then started singing
LO LO LO LO LOLA, which
sounded great coming from the
Holte End. Lola quickly
scampered back to the seat with
Ruby, her name echoing round
the ground.

Now she snuggled back under
Ruby's cardigan so
the steward would not
see her. United
players were not

happy and surrounded the Ref, but the Ref waved play on. Then came the icing on the cake with Grealish scoring the winning goal. The crowd again went potty and Lola and Ruby joined them singing his name GREALISH, GREALISH.

At the end of the game, Grealish came over to them and gave Ruby his shirt. She said "Thank you." He said "That's the least I can do." Lola said to Ruby "You're blushing". She said "Don't be silly" (Mind you she did feel a warm glow on her face). Lola and Ruby skipped to the Villa Shop. Ruby took her cardigan off to show her Villa Shirt with her name on the back. She said to the assistant. "Can I please have the new Villa Shirt with Grandad printed on the back."

They had a great time.
CHEERS GRANDAD

RUBY AND LOLA AT NAN AND GRANDADS

by
Grandad Craig Hookway

Ruby and Lola were stopping at Nanny and Grandads for the weekend, while Ruby's Mom and Dad went for a Spa Break.

Grandad was in his shed, or 'man cave' as he liked to call it. Nanny had made him a cup of tea. Ruby said "can I take it to him," "of course you can" said Nanny, "but don't drop it, that's his favourite Villa mug. Lola, you can carry the M&S Digestive biscuits, also his favourite."

The man cave looked like a log cabin from the front with two double glazed windows. Nan said "Grandad is always making tables out of old pallets, he makes lots of things in there." They all sat  down on the bench in the shed and Grandad drank his tea. Ruby saw the dartboard and said "can we play darts please." Grandad said "ok, but we can't leave Nanny out, she used to be good at darts." So Ruby called Nan. "Come on we are playing darts, Lola and me versus you two." Ruby threw first, she got off to a good start scoring 41, then Nan had her go and scored 60, well you could see why Nan had all them trophy's from when she was playing for the local social club. Lola had her go and scored 100, GREAT SCORE. Lola eventually went on to win the game with a double top check out, finishing like a true pro. Ruby said "Get in, Well done, Yippee, is there anything that you can't do." Lola purred with a smug grin, Grandad said "well played, shall we have a BBQ now." They all shouted "YEAY that would be nice."

So Grandad set up the BBQ, while Nanny sorted the food out. They had black crispy sausages (ok burnt) burgers and kebab skewers, which

were lovely. When they had finished eating, Grandad fell asleep in his reclining chair.

Just out of curiosity Ruby and Lola went back into the shed. They looked around and saw lots of interesting things, but there was one box that stood out, it was a red box, on the top shelf. Lola jumped up to get it. Lola said "It has a blue ribbon round it and says do not open." Lola looked up the garden and saw Grandad still asleep, they could not resist it, so they opened it and with a puff of smoke, dust and stars, out popped a grey rabbit. He said "my

name is Deano, named after Dean Saunders the Villa player that scored in the League Cup Final against Manchester United." Ruby said "did Jack Grealish play in that game." "You're blushing again" said Lola.

Ruby thought, is this a dream?

Ruby could tell his name was Deano by his big gold collar with his name on it, which he wore around his neck.

Ruby introduced herself and Lola.

Deano said "Nice to meet you, do you fancy a bit of excitement?"

Ruby and Lola both said "Yes". "Right then Ruby get on my back and hold on to my collar. Lola you put your paws around Ruby's waist and hold on tight." said Deano. Then all of a sudden, Deano ran out of the shed up the path and they took off into the air. Ruby and Lola shouted "WOW" Ruby's tummy rolled, as if she was in a car going over a massive bridge. They were starting to pick up speed now, Deano's ears were pinned back against his head and Rubys long hair was blowing in Lola's face. Lola's tail was wagging everywhere in the

wind. They were going up and down, Lola thought she was going to be sick at one point.
Ruby said "OMG this is fun." Lola said "There is a crow following us and catching up fast." The crow got to within inches of Lola's tail and was squawking like mad. Ruby thought, was this a good idea after all? Deano said "Don't worry, I have this covered, hang on tight". They were heading towards a big branch on the tree in Nanny and Grandad's garden. Deano said "Right here we go, hold on as tight as you can." Lola and Ruby both shouted "No'oooooo"

and with that they all nose dived under the branch, leaving the crow to crash into the tree, and then fly away very slowly.

Ruby thought PHEW that was a close shave. She opened her eyes and was lying on Grandad's lap. Lola was on Nanny's lap, having some fuss.

Well, what a day that was.

Thanks Nanny and Grandad.

Ruby and Lola`s weekend in the caravan with Grandma and Grandpa

by
Grandad Craig Hookway

Ruby and Lola's weekend in the caravan with Grandma and Grandpa

Grandma and Grandpa have a mobile caravan and use it to go away for mini breaks to the countryside.

They asked Ruby and Lola if they would like to come, they said that would be lovely.

They decided to go to the peak district Derbyshire.

Grandpa packed the car and caravan, not forgetting the bowls and badminton kit, Grandma sorted out the food.

Grandma said "do you like marmalade on your toast for breakfast?" Lola shouted "mmmm yes please, thank you Grandma" while Ruby sat on the chair watching TV drinking pop and eating biscuits.

1

Ruby and Lola`s weekend in the caravan with Grandma and Grandpa

Grandpa said, "ok, all packed now" so Lola and Ruby got in the car. Grandma put their seat belts on, Grandpa checked the map and off they went.

The traffic was not too bad for a Friday afternoon and in less than two hours they arrived at the camp site. Grandpa parked up and said, "Right Ruby and Lola can you wind the legs down on the caravan and fill the water container please," Grandpa showed them how to do the first leg on the caravan, then they were fine after that. They went to get the water which was over by the farmhouse, the container was on wheels so it was easy to transport. While they were waiting for it to fill Ruby saw a lady come out of the farm house, she came over to them and said "Hello, are you stopping for the weekend" Lola said "Yes we are staying with Grandma and Grandpa in that caravan over there." The nice lady said "that's a nice caravan, my name is Alice, If you want anything over the weekend come and see me, I also have a little shop which opens at 8 o'clock in the morning" Ruby and Lola thanked Alice and thought what a nice lady as they went back to the caravan.

The surrounding fields of the campsite had sheep, horses, cows and the view was gorgeous, Grandma had picked a good site and there was a pub across the road, what more could you ask for. Grandpa suggested they all go over for a drink, Lola said "sounds fun." The pub was an old country pub with oak beams and a pool table. They sat down with their drinks and Grandpa said "who wants a game of pool?" Lola was first to shout up "MEEEEE" Lola seemed really up for it, so Ruby let Lola play on her own while she chatted to Grandma. Lola put the money in, set the balls up and tossed a coin to see who would break. Grandpa said "heads" and won the toss, he decided to let Lola break so Lola put some chalk on the tip of her cue, broke the pack and one of the striped balls went in the middle pocket, then potted another four on the bounce, Grandpa was shocked on how good Lola was, he came back and potted five on the trot. In the end it came down to both needing the black to win, Ruby said to Grandma "lets watch the end of the game, it looks close." Lola was next to go but she missed her shot. Lola said "OMG." With Grandpa lining up his shot, other people took interest. Lola said "no pressure" then he chalked his cue, took a swig of his drink, then took aim, pulled the cue back and bang the black ball went straight into the pocket. Lola congratulated Grandpa, shaking his hand with her paw. Then just as they were about to sit down noticed the white ball still moving and going towards the pocket, there was a slope on the pool table and the people who had took an interest were still watching, they were locals so knew what was going to happen. They were going ORRRRRR, the white ball slowly rolled into the pocket, it seemed that half the pub was watching as there was a roar when the white ball dropped in. Grandpa was in disbelief. Mind you so was Lola, more from the noise made by the people watching. So this time Grandpa shook Lola`s paw and said "well played" they sat down to a round of applause. After that they drank up and made there way back to the caravan. Grandma made some warm milk for Lola and Ruby had hot chocolate, Grandma and Grandpa had coffee and they all had a biscuit. It was a lovely evening with a clear blue sky so they

Ruby and Lola's weekend in the caravan with Grandma and Grandpa

sat outside to watch the sun go down over the hills, Grandma said "it should be a nice day tomorrow, red sky at night shepherds delight." When the sun had gone down, Ruby said to Grandma "I am tired now can I go to bed" Grandma said "ok let me go and make your bed up." As she did that Lola and Ruby gave Grandpa a kiss and cuddle and said "goodnight." They snuggled up in bed and Grandma read them a bed time story. Ruby and Lola slowly dropped off to sleep.

The next morning, the sun was rising, it was lovely, you could just see it through the misty window, so Lola wiped it with her head "that's better" she said.

Grandma was up and about, she said "do you two want marmalade on toast for breakfast" Ruby and Lola both nodded "yes please". As it was a nice day they sat at a table outside enjoying the view. After they had finished Grandma said "we are short on milk can you two go and get some from the shop please" Ruby said "ok, no problem, Lola we may meet that nice lady called Alice again" so off they went.

When they got to the farmyard Ruby opened the gate and put the catch back on so the animals could not escape. Lola saw Alice in the shop, Ruby asked her "can we have some milk please?" "yes of course you can, would you like fresh milk?" "Have you ever milked a cow before?" said Alice. Ruby and Lola said "no."

"Would you like to" said Alice " That sounds fun." said Lola." They walked through the back into the field where they could see Grandma waving at them, so they waved back.

Alice said "this is Daisy the cow, we get our milk from her for the shop." Alice went and got two bottles to put the milk in. Alice said "you watch me then you can have a go," she pulled the udders softly with the milk going into the bottle. "Here Ruby, you can have a go now." Ruby got hold of the bottle and started pulling the udder, it did not work at first. Alice said "squeeze a bit harder." Then the milk started to come out. When the bottle was full it was

Lola`s turn, Lola picked up the bottle with one paw and the udder with the other, "it's working, it's like magic" she said. When the bottle was full Lola put a top on it. "Would you like a bag?" said Alice "yes please Alice" said Lola They thanked Alice. "It was my pleasure" said Alice. Ruby and Lola made their way back. Passing through the farmyard, they saw a dog in his kennel with his name above the door, it was Coco, "that's a lovely name" said Ruby. Coco opened one eye and said "hello, what are you doing here? I am trying to sleep." Ruby said "we have just got some milk from Daisy." "Oh, that silly cow" said Coco. Ruby said "that's not nice, why do you call her that?" "well when I am rounding up the sheep all I can hear is her laughing at me, especially when the sheep don't do as they are told." The ducks and chickens then started laughing, Coco said "now look what you've done" Lola said "WHOOPS."

"Now if you don't mind I have some sleep to catch up on." said Coco, at that he said goodbye and closed his eyes.

They got back to the caravan gave Grandma the milk and then they all got in the car, Grandpa said "we are going for a walk on the Tissington trail, alongside the river, up to the stepping stones, then have a picnic."

"Sounds fun" said Lola. When they got

there they put on their walking boots and put the picnic in the rucksack.

The river was very clear, you could see the fish. One of them winked at Ruby as he went past. It was a pleasant walk, there were a few walkers passing them, some had walking sticks and there were dogs having great fun in the water chasing sticks.

By the time they got to the stepping stones the sun was blazing hot so they all sat on the grass to have their picnic. Lola and Ruby had some pop and cake, then went down to the stepping stones to see if they could get to the other side of the river. Lola found it easy to get to the other side "it was like playing hop scotch for me"

said Lola. Then out the corner of her eye Ruby saw that fish again, this time Ruby winked at the fish, so the fish stopped and said "you're not going to try and catch us with a fishing net like the other little girls?" Ruby said "No, anyway what's your name?" The fish replied "Ted."
Ruby decided it was that hot that she would take her socks and boots off and sit down on the big stone and dangle her feet in the water, Ted started to rub up against Ruby`s feet, this tickled Ruby and made her laugh so much that she nearly fell in the water. Lola came running back to save her "thank you Lola, I thought I was going to get wet then." said Ruby.
Then Ruby heard Ted say "see ya,

going to catch up with my family" Ruby waved goodbye.

Ruby and Lola went back up to Grandpa and Grandma. They said "shall we make our way back now." When they got back to the caravan Lola and Ruby were tired and went to bed, after some hot chocolate.

The Sunday morning was again nice and warm and after breakfast Grandpa said "would anyone like a game of bowls?" Everyone said yes. It was a close game with Grandma eventually winning, good old Grandma still got it.

Ruby could see the sheep running around and went over to the fence to see what all the fuss was about. It was Coco rounding up the sheep and yep Daisy the cow was laughing her head

off, the chickens and ducks also joined in. Coco looked up and shouted in an out of breath voice "told you it was true,"
Coco had done a great job for the farmer getting all the sheep together. It started to rain and Grandma called Ruby and Lola back to the caravan. As the forecast was not good for the rest of the weekend they thought the best option was to head back home.
Lola and Ruby wound the legs back up on the caravan, Grandpa hooked the caravan on to the car, Grandma put their seat belts on and they were off. After about twenty minutes into the journey it started to rain again with loud thunder and lighting. Good idea to go home, typical English weather.

Ruby and Lola`s weekend in the caravan with Grandma and Grandpa

On this weekend Ruby and Lola had met some lovely people and animals, especially Coco.

Thank you
GRANDMA AND GRANDPA
xxx

THE BEST MOMMY AND DADDY

by
Grandad Craig Hookway

"Good morning Ruby, what would you like to do today?" Said mommy. "Can we go into London to buy new dresses for both of us, then we could wear them for the Tokio Myers concert tonight at the O2 arena."

Tokio Myers played the piano and is Ben's favourite performer. Ben is also very good on the piano.

Ben is Ruby`s big brother who had gone to work with Daddy today.

Lola`s ears popped up, she then ran into the lounge and said "did I hear you say you are going into London town centre." "Yes that's right said

THE BEST MOMMY AND DADDY

Mommy" Lola said "Can I come as well please." "Of course you can" replied mommy. So they had breakfast and made  their way to the station, it was only a 30 minute journey to the town centre on the train. They got off at Trafalgar Square, where they saw Nelson's Column. They went over to have a closer look at the bottom of the column. There was a big lion painted black, where they had their picture taken. There was also a big fountain close by and as it was a hot day Mommy suggested shall we go and get an ice cream and eat it while dangling our feet in the fountain. "mmmm! that sounds lovely" said Lola. Lola`s ice cream was melting quicker than she  could eat it and was getting in a right mess. Mommy had a tissue and wiped her face, that's better. Some of the children were paddling in the water having fun. When they finished their ice cream they headed off to find a dress, they ended up in Harrods.

Harrods was an impressive store to say the least, steeped in history. They made their way to the ladies clothes section. There were lots of dresses for Mommy to look at. Ruby said to Mommy "Can Lola and I go and look in the children's section please." "Yes you  can, I will catch up with you in a bit, replied Mommy." Lola said "come on this way." When they got there Ruby and Lola were amazed at all the lovely things there.

There was a walk in dolls house, some electric cars big enough to sit in, teddy bears, dolls large and small, Lego bricks the size of house bricks. Ruby went to the dolls house first, it had a thatched roof and a black door. When they opened the door it creaked, the inside had wooden beams, two chairs, a table, with three bowls of porridge on it. They both had one spoonful of the

porridge, it was not too hot or cold it was just right especially with the honey on the top, so they scoffed the lot "mmmmmm that was nice," said Lola. Ruby thought of the story Goldilocks and the Three Bears. Ruby saw that Lola had porridge on her whiskers which looked funny, so said nothing.

They left the dolls house and saw the electric cars, there was an open top BMW which looked gorgeous. Lola said "Come on we are going for a spin.  So they jumped in with Lola at the wheel. "Belt up, here we go" said Lola. They saw a door open and headed to where the warehouse was, it was a big open space, so Lola went a bit faster. Ruby saw some cats then looked behind and there was one on their tail, so Lola went even faster. Lola said to herself "Wow this baby can move." There was a crowd starting to develop. The cats on one side of the warehouse and the mice on the other. The cat did not want to harm them, he just wanted to race them.

They had done three laps of the warehouse, Ruby said "make this the last lap Mommy will wonder where we are." Lola saw  the door open, where they came in, they were in the final straight, the cat was coming up on the inside, Lola floored it to increase the lead. The mice had found a chequered flag and waved it as they went past them cheering YEAH well done. They went through the door very slowly, parked up and went and found Mommy.

"Hi Mommy, how are you? got a dress yet?" said Ruby. "Yes" said

Mommy, "now let's get you one. Oh Lola come here, what have you got on your whiskers? Let me wipe your face." Ruby had a

smile on her face. They then went to the children's section where they found a beautiful red dress which fitted perfect, paid for it and made their way home.

Daddy and Ben were already home and were getting ready to go out tonight. Ruby said "Mommy and I have new dresses to wear tonight." Mommy and Ruby put their new dresses on. Daddy said "You two look gorgeous."

They arrived at the 02 Arena, it was full. Tokio Myers was very popular especially in London as he was born there.

He was due to come on stage at 7.30pm, it was now 8.00pm and no sign of him. The crowd were getting restless, then there was an announcement. Unfortunately Tokio is unwell and cannot perform. Ben could hear some people in the crowd saying we have come all this way for nothing, and were starting to leave.
 The stage looked very inviting with all the equipment and bright lights. Ben looked at Ruby and quietly said

THE BEST MOMMY AND DADDY

"Shall we" with
that they ran on to
the stage. Ben
found the piano and
Ruby the
microphone.

Mommy said to
Daddy "this will be interesting,"
Lola said to Mommy "don't worry
they have been practising together."
Ruby tapped the mic, "testing 1,2,3."
Daddy smiled. Ben said "ok on 3"
and they started.
The first song they chose to play was
'Don't Look Back in Anger' by
OASIS. Ben played the intro to this,
it was lovely. Ruby's timing was
spot on. This was for their Aunty
Sally, Daddies Sister. It was quite

appropriate, as the crowd started to come back in. So they played another one, this time they toned it down a bit with Elton Johns'

'A Candle in the Wind, which Ben sang on his own. Everyone was back in now and quiet, listening to Ben. At the end everyone clapped and shouted "More"! so Ben said "ok one more," and Yep you guessed it. It was RUBY, RUBY, RUBY, RUBY! by the Kaiser Chiefs. This time the crowd started to sing along to the chorus, jumping up and down, including Mommy, Daddy and Lola. At the end Ruby and Ben got a rapturous applause. Daddy shouted "Take a bow you two."

When they got back to Mommy and Daddy they both got big hugs. "That was brilliant" said Mommy, "everyone was saying well done." On the way out Daddy spoke to a man in black trousers and shirt with black hair. He was called Simon, he said "Are these two with you." Daddy replied "Yes." Simon said "Here is my card, give me a ring tomorrow." "Sure will" said Daddy.

They had all
enjoyed
themselves.
What a great day.

Thank you Mommy and Daddy.
You're **Simply the Best.**

Ruby Leigh and Lola
Visit the Garden Centre

by
Grandad Craig Hookway

Ruby and Lola decided to go to Auntie Sheila`s with Nanny, as they had not seen Sheila for some time.

They jumped in the car with Nanny and off they went. When they got there Sheila gave everybody a big hug and made a drink for everyone.

While they were sitting there chatting Lola noticed another cat, fast asleep, even snoring sometimes. Lola asked "who's that" Sheila said "that is Poppy having her afternoon nap."

Poppy lifted one eye to see who

was there then closed it and carried on sleeping.

While chatting, Auntie Sheila said "do you fancy going to the garden centre across the road" Nanny said "that would be nice, I need some more plants for the garden."

Poppy then woke up and said "Can I come, I fancy an afternoon stroll" Auntie Sheila said "Of course you can."

Poppy then stood up, but when she stood up, she did not seem to stop, she just got bigger and bigger, "You're a big girl" said Lola "yep" said. Poppy.

They got to the garden centre and found lots of flowers in full bloom, there  was a lovely smell and lots of people there. As Auntie Sheila and Nanny were looking at the plants together Ruby Leigh said "Can we catch up with you later" Nanny said "ok but be good though" "Of course we will" said Lola with a rye smile, so the three of them carried on walking where they came across a garden gnome all on his own. Ruby Leigh said "Ahh look, he only has one ear." The gnome

said "I can still hear
you though, please
don't pick me up like
the last little boy did
and used me like a football."
"Of course I won`t, is that how
you lost your ear?" "Yes" said
the gnome "that is the reason I
have been stuck here all
summer, nobody wants to buy a
gnome with one ear, all my
gnome friends have gone to nice
homes." "What's your name"
said Ruby Leigh. "Pardon" said
the gnome. "I said what's your
name" saying it a little bit louder
"Oh my name is Ron, no need to

4

shout" said Ron. Ron looked up and up and yes he was looking at Poppy "you're tall" said Ron. Ruby Leigh said "Come on walk round with us you can show us round." "Ok" said Ron "that would be nice."

Ron led them to the big pond where some of his friends were there. He saw Lilley the toad, they had been good friends for some time. Lilley had escaped the fishing net a few times, from that same little boy who had used Ron as a football. Lilley liked swimming in the pond especially on hot days like today. Ron could not swim. Lilley saw Ron and swam towards him

"Hi Ron, it's a lovely day today, what you up to?" "I am showing my new friends around the garden centre" said Ron, "Oh that's great, have fun" replied Lilley and carried on swimming. Ron turned round to Poppy, Lola and Ruby Leigh to say "Come on lets go on the bridge." Then out of nowhere came that little boy and kicked Ron into the air over the pond, Poppy thought, oh no, he can't swim, Poppy ran

round the side of the
pond and dived in, to
try and catch Ron.
Poppy managed to
stop Ron getting wet
but could not hold on to him,
Ron flew back into the air again.
Auntie Sheila saw what was
happening and ran down the
slope to catch Ron and said to
him "You're coming home with
me, even with one ear." Ron just
smiled with glee, feeling really
happy inside, to the extent a
little tear dropped from Ron's
eye.
Ruby Leigh and Lola helped
Poppy out of the water, they

both said "Well done, you saved Ron from drowning," Poppy said "Cheers, I move quite quick for a fat cat." Ruby Leigh and Lola laughed but stopped when Poppy shook her whole body to get rid of the water off her fur, now Ruby Leigh and Lola were wet and Poppy was laughing. Then they heard a voice, it was Ron with a big smile on his face, he shouted "Come on its time to go home and I am coming with you." All three of them cheered. "Yeah that's great, do we get a discount because you only have one ear"

said Lola jokingly.
"Hey said Ron." "Oh
it does not matter."
said Lola.
So they all went home
happy, Ron with Poppy and
Auntie Sheila. Ron's bed was
right next to Poppies and he had
to put up with the snoring, but
did not mind one bit.

Thank you for a lovely day out
NANNY

Printed in Great Britain
by Amazon

54291399R00037